party bag

happy birthday

For my Ollie, whose hiccuppy moments inspired this story – P...

For Mum and Dad, and India, my own Baby Bear – L.J.

First published 2008 by Macmillan Children's Books
a division of Macmillan Publishers Limited
The Macmillan Building, 4 Crinan Street, London N1 9XW
Basingstoke and Oxford
Associated companies throughout the world
www.panmacmillan.com

ISBN: 978-0-230-53029-4 (HB)
ISBN: 978-0-230-53176-5 (PB)

Text copyright © Penny Little 2008
Illustrations copyright © Lara Jones 2008
Moral rights asserted.

1 3 5 7 9 8 6 4 2

A CIP catalogue record for this book is available from the British Library.

Printed in Belgium

Penny Little   Lara Jones

Baby Bear's Birthday Hiccups

MACMILLAN CHILDREN'S BOOKS

It was Baby Bear's birthday, and his party was almost over. He had opened **all** his presents, blown out **all** his birthday candles and had **two** pieces of birthday cake.

"Come on everyone, time for one last party game!"
said Mummy Bear.
"Hooray!" everyone cried.

But Baby Bear went . . .

"You've got hiccups!" said Mummy Bear.
She rubbed his tummy,
and patted his back.

Pat
Pat
Pat

"All gone?" she asked.

"Hic!"

went Baby Bear.

"Goodness me," said Mummy Bear.
"What will we do?"

"I know the purrrrrrfect cure for hiccups,"

said Little Leopard, pouncing up.

"Tickling!

And I'm a verrrrry good tickler."

So he wriggled his little paws and
began to tickle Baby Bear all over.
"Stopppp!" squealed Baby Bear, as he wriggled and giggled.

"All gone?" smiled Little Leopard.

"Hic!"

gasped Baby Bear.

"Try holding your breath like me," huffed Little Hippo.
"Holding your breath always works."

Baby Bear took a gigantic gulp of air . . .

"Huuuup!"

He waited . . .

and waited . . .

and waited . . .

"Oh dear," whispered Little Hippo.

"Hey Baby Bear, there's only one cure for hiccups,"
grinned Little Monkey cheekily.
"The MONKEY Cure! It's easy peasy, just watch me!

You stand on one leg . . .

. . . hop up and down.

Close one eye . . .

and pat your tummy.

All at once!"

But it wasn't as easy as it looked.
"Hic!" wobbled Baby Bear.

"What you need is to calm down," said Nanny Giraffe softly.

"And Nanny Giraffe's kisses are the cure for hiccups."

She bent down low and gave Baby Bear . . .

one
two
three

big kisses!

"All gone?" soothed Nanny Giraffe.
"Hic!" went Baby Bear.

Suddenly he felt very sleepy.
He was about to let out
a tiny yawn when . . .

RRR

"My Dad says a grrrrrreat big scary surprise always gets rid of hiccups!" grinned Little Lion.

Everybody looked at Baby Bear and waited . . .

ROOARR!

and waited . . .

"Hic!"

went Baby Bear.

"Oh **dear**," said Mummy Bear. "WHAT shall we do with my hiccupy bear?"

But it was time for everyone to go home.

Baby Bear's friends put on their hats and buttoned up their coats and Mummy Bear gave them each a party bag.

But Baby Bear felt sad. Would nothing *ever* stop his hiccups?
Then he heard a voice that made him smile . . .

"THERE you are, Little Birthday Bear," said Daddy Bear, scooping him up.

"Hic!"
grinned Baby Bear.

"Ah!" said Daddy Bear. "Time for
a drink and a cuddle, I think."

Baby Bear snuggled deeply
into Daddy Bear's arms.
It was very comfy.
He sipped his water slowly

And very soon, it seemed, Baby Bear's hiccups became smaller . . . "Hic!"

and smaller . . . "Hic!"

and smaller . . . "Hic!"

Until at last they disappeared.
But Baby Bear didn't even notice . . .

because he was already **fast asleep.**